The Boxcar Children® Mysteries

THE CANOE TRIP MYSTERY

created by
GERTRUDE CHANDLER WARNER

Illustrated by Charles Tang

ALBERT WHITMAN & Company
Morton Grove, Illinois

Library of Congress Cataloging-in-Publication Data
Warner, Gertrude Chandler, 1890-
The canoe trip mystery / created by Gertrude Chandler Warner;
illustrated by Charles Tang.
p. cm. — (The Boxcar children mysteries)
Summary: While canoeing and backpacking near Timberwolf Lake, the
Aldens receive strange warnings to stay away from the area and stumble
upon clues to a missing cache of stolen coins.
ISBN 0-8075-1058-0 (hardcover).
ISBN 0-8075-1059-9 (paperback).
[1. Camping–Fiction. 2. Mystery and detective stories.]
I. Tang, Charles, ill. II. Title. III. Series: Warner, Gertrude
Chandler, 1890-   Boxcar children mysteries.
PZ7.W244Can   1994   94-4102
[Fic]–dc20   CIP
                                         AC

Contents

CHAPTER 1

Angela

One warm spring morning, the four Alden children were outside their home in Greenfield. They loaded two tents, four backpacks, and a first-aid kit into their grandfather's station wagon.

Their dog, Watch, woke up from his nap and ran to the car wagging his tail.

"No, Watch, I'm afraid you're staying here." Fourteen-year-old Henry Alden patted the dog's soft fur. "We have so much equipment to take. You wouldn't even have room to stretch."

"We're not going to have much room either," Henry's six-year-old brother, Benny, said as he raced Watch back to the house. Benny wanted to see what the housekeeper, Mrs. McGregor, was putting in the large waterproof pack. "Mmmm, fresh homemade bread." Benny sniffed the open bag with delight.

"Are you sure we'll have enough food to last a whole week?" Benny asked his two older sisters, Jessie and Violet. They were carrying a bag of cooking utensils between them.

"Don't worry, Benny," his oldest sister, Jessie, answered. Jessie was twelve and very responsible.

Ten-year-old Violet added a drawing pad and some pencils to her backpack, which was already in the back of the car. "I know we shouldn't take too many things on a canoe," Violet said apologetically to Henry.

"Don't worry, Violet. Your sketch pad hardly weighs anything, and we know how much you like to draw." Henry smiled at his sister.

"Are you almost ready?" the children's grandfather asked as he walked out of the house. "I told Aunt Jane we would meet her at Ernie's Sporting Goods Store in Silver Falls at nine o'clock. I don't want to keep her waiting."

"We're just checking to make sure we haven't forgotten anything," Jessie answered.

Grandfather smiled fondly at his four grandchildren. He would miss them while they went canoeing and backpacking for a week with their Aunt Jane. But he wouldn't worry about them.

His grandchildren were used to looking after themselves. After their parents died, they had lived on their own in a boxcar until he found them and gave them a home.

Mrs. McGregor helped Jessie and Violet put the last bag in the car. Then she waved good-bye. Watch ran from one child to another before he obediently followed Mrs. McGregor back to the house.

The Aldens arrived in Silver Falls in

plenty of time to meet Aunt Jane. Grandfather parked the station wagon right on bustling Main Street. Silver Falls was an old New England town right next to Elmford, where Aunt Jane lived. Large maple and oak trees shaded the low storefront buildings.

"Look, isn't that Aunt Jane's car?" Jessie asked, pointing to a blue convertible.

"Yes," Grandfather answered. "She must already be in Ernie's store."

Ernie's Sporting Goods Store was in a big old sandstone building just off Main Street. The Aldens walked through a room filled with bicycles and fishing poles. They found Ernie setting up a sailboat display in the boat room.

"So, today's the big day." Ernie smiled at the children. "Just think, in a few hours, you'll all be paddling on Timberwolf Lake."

"Not me, I'm afraid," Grandfather answered his good friend. "I'm getting a little too old for long canoe trips. The children are going with their Aunt Jane."

"I know. She stopped in the store earlier this morning, but left to pick up something. She said it was a surprise." Ernie winked at the children. "She should be back soon."

Ernie had been helping Aunt Jane and the children plan their trip for more than a month now. He had also taken the children out for little canoe trips to give them some lessons. Henry and Jessie had learned very quickly. Aunt Jane was already an experienced canoeist.

Ernie advised the Aldens on the sleeping bags, lightweight canoes, life preservers, and paddles they would need to rent for their trip.

"Why do we need two canoes?" Benny asked.

"It's not safe for more than four people to be in a canoe," Violet answered.

"Whose canoe will I be in?" Benny wanted to know.

"Well, to start, I thought maybe you and Jessie could be in Aunt Jane's canoe," Henry answered. "I'll take Violet in mine. We can always change later in the trip."

"I'm sure any boat would be glad to have

you as a passenger, Benny," Ernie said, rumpling Benny's hair.

"See, Benny, here's where we'll be going," Henry said, unfolding one of his many maps and holding it out to show his brother. "Grandfather will drive all of us to this park," Henry continued, pointing to Wolverine State Park. "We'll unload all the canoeing equipment there and get right on Timberwolf Lake."

"Timberwolf Lake," Benny repeated.

"Yes, and we're also going to canoe on Catfish Lake." Henry pointed on the map. "Then we'll meet Grandfather in a town called White Pine."

Henry and Benny were very busy looking at the map. They did not notice the tall blonde woman in her late twenties who was listening to every word they said. The woman wore turquoise designer jeans, jade earrings, and an expensive jacket. She seemed nervous when Ernie came up to ask her if she wanted to rent a canoe.

"No, I certainly do not need any canoeing equipment. I've been canoeing for years and

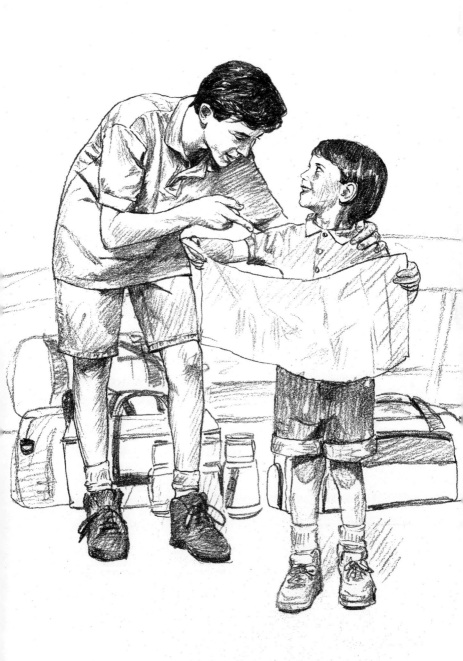

have just bought myself a brand-new canoe." She sounded smug.

"Besides," the woman continued, "I don't believe in renting outdoor equipment." She looked pointedly at the rented canoes the Aldens had picked out. "You never know what you're getting when you rent."

"What a snob," Jessie whispered to Henry. Henry nodded.

"But there is something I do need." The tall blonde woman beckoned to Ernie. "I need a topographic map of Royal National Park."

"Topo . . . what?" Benny whispered loudly to Jessie.

"It's a map that shows you the shape of the land — the hills, valleys — " Jessie began.

"You really can't go canoeing without one," the woman interrupted. "It also shows you where waterfalls and rapids are."

"I'll go find a sales clerk in our map department who can help you," Ernie told the woman politely.

As soon as Ernie had left, the woman turned to the Aldens. She extended her hand to Jessie. "I'm Angela Tripp," she said.

"I'm Jessie Alden." Jessie shook her hand. "And these are my brothers, Henry and Benny, and my sister, Violet."

"I couldn't help overhearing your canoeing plans," Angela said. "I'm surprised you would want to canoe on Timberwolf Lake this time of year. There are such bad thunderstorms up there now."

"Really? The late spring is supposed to be a very good time to go canoeing," Henry answered.

"If it does rain a lot, we have waterproof tents and rainwear with us," Jessie added. She was always very practical.

Angela sighed. "Well, I suppose you know that wolves live near Timberwolf Lake. That's how it got its name."

"Wolves," Benny repeated. His eyes grew rounder.

"Yes," Angela said. "And you know wolves hunt at night."

Henry cleared his throat. "I'm pretty sure there are no wolves in that part of New England," he said.

"Well, you'll be very far from people up there. No one will be able to help you if you are attacked by a wild animal," Angela snapped. She did not even try to look friendly anymore. When the salesman came to help her buy a map, she turned away from the Aldens and did not say another word to them.

"She's not very nice," Benny said, after Angela Tripp left the store.

"I don't understand why she was trying to scare you like that," Grandfather said, when the children told Ernie and him about their conversation with Angela.

"You certainly won't have to worry about wolves," Ernie said, shaking his head.

"There haven't been wild wolves in that part of New England for over a hundred years," Grandfather said firmly. "I used to canoe on Timberwolf Lake as a boy. The weather up there isn't any worse than it is down here," he added.

"I can't help thinking she might have had a reason for not wanting us to go on our canoe trip," Violet said quietly.

"Maybe we'll have a mystery to solve," Benny said just as Aunt Jane walked in the store with her husband, Andy Bean.

Uncle Andy and Aunt Jane gave each of the children a great big bear hug. "We did a little last-minute shopping for the trip," Aunt Jane said. She smiled at her nieces and nephews. She always enjoyed being with them. They would be good company while her husband was away on a business trip.

"Can we open them now?" Benny asked, looking at the wrapped presents Uncle Andy had handed each of the children.

"Certainly," Aunt Jane said. She led them to a shady courtyard outside the back of the store. The Aldens all sat at a large picnic table and opened their presents.

"Yum," Benny said happily. His gift was

a bag of trail mix — nuts, dried fruit, and chocolate bits.

Henry received a Swiss army knife. It had a can opener, a bottle opener, and several other tools all folded up inside it.

Jessie received a compass.

Violet opened her present last. She pulled a tin camping cup out of its box. "Thank you, Aunt Jane," she said, smiling.

When all the excitement over the presents had died down, Aunt Jane turned to Jessie. "Now, what's all this I heard you saying about a mystery?" she asked.

As the children told their aunt all about Angela, Henry began to frown. He was worried about Angela. Who was she? he wondered. And why was she trying to scare them?

CHAPTER 2

All Aboard!

Ernie and Aunt Jane attached the two canoes and the paddles to the roof of the car. Henry and Jessie squeezed the sleeping bags and life preservers into the back.

Then Aunt Jane, Uncle Andy, and the Aldens stopped for an early lunch at Piccolos' Pizzeria. The Aldens had a large Pizza Supreme topped with cheese, sausage, mushrooms, green peppers, and Mrs. Piccolo's special tomato sauce.

At the next table, two men were talking

very loudly. "I can't believe someone broke into the museum and then didn't take anything," one of the men said.

"It *is* strange," the other man answered. "The burglars only disturbed the coin collection. They didn't even bother with the jewelry or antique silver." Both men shook their heads.

"Did you hear that?" Benny asked Mrs. Piccolo. She was busy refilling Grandfather's cup of coffee.

"Yes," Mrs. Piccolo answered. "It's good nothing was taken this time. About a year ago, a large private coin collection was stolen from a local man named Orville Withington."

"I think I remember reading about that," Grandfather said. "They never caught the burglars."

"No." Mrs. Piccolo shook her head. "They never did."

"Maybe the same people broke into the museum," Violet said.

"Yes, but if they did, why didn't they take anything?" Jessie asked.

"I'm afraid you won't have time to solve this mystery," Grandfather said, knowing what they were thinking. "You'll be far away from any burglars on your canoe trail."

"Speaking of the canoe trail, I think we should be on our way," Aunt Jane reminded Grandfather gently. "We'd like to make a good start this afternoon and get to the first campsite before dark."

Uncle Andy looked at his watch. "From here, the drive to Wolverine State Park should only take about two hours. You should be on the lake by three in the afternoon," he told his wife.

"It stays light late now," Violet reminded her aunt. "We'll have time."

Grandfather paid the bill. Everyone except Uncle Andy piled into the station wagon. He stood and waved as they drove off.

On the outskirts of Silver Falls, they passed big red barns, potato fields, and small towns with low brick buildings. Farther and farther north, the children began to see pine forests. Timberwolf Lake shone in the distance.

"Oh, it's so beautiful up here," Violet said.

"The air smells so fresh," Henry added.

"Grandfather, we have to turn at the next junction," Jessie said, looking at the map. Grandfather turned onto a wide dirt road and followed the signs to Wolverine State Park. He stopped the car in front of a dock on Timberwolf Lake and helped his grandchildren and Aunt Jane unload all their equipment.

Everyone was busy. First Henry and Aunt Jane took the canoes off the top of the car and carried them to the water. Grandfather put the paddles and tents inside them. Benny carefully carried the waterproof bags of food from the car. Jessie and Violet packed the sleeping bags, life preservers, food bags, backpacks, and first-aid kit into the canoes. They were careful to put an equal load in each one.

Henry tied a long piece of rope to the front of each canoe. Jessie and Violet pushed both canoes into the water, while Henry and Aunt Jane held the ropes and walked the canoes toward the dock.

Benny took off his sneakers and socks and dipped his toes in the water. "Ooh, it's cold!" he cried.

"The water hasn't had time to warm up yet. It's only spring," Violet said gently. She felt sorry for her brother. She knew how much he wanted to go swimming.

"Benny, you won't have to get your feet wet if you get into the canoe from the dock," Jessie said as she tied the canoe lines to the dock.

Henry and Aunt Jane got into the canoes first and tried to hold them steady. With Grandfather's help, Violet carefully climbed into Henry's canoe. Jessie and Benny joined Aunt Jane.

Grandfather untied the canoes and threw the ropes to Henry and Aunt Jane. "Good-bye," he waved. "I'll meet you at the dock in White Pine in a week."

"Good-bye, Grandfather," his grandchildren called loudly. Benny waved. He was the only one not paddling. But he sat very still in the middle of the canoe, watching Jessie paddle in front of him. Aunt Jane sat behind Benny, steering with her paddle.

Aunt Jane took the lead and the two canoes moved slowly across the lake.

Pine and birch trees lined both sides of the rocky shore. Canadian geese flew overhead. The still, blue lake stretched ahead of the canoeists for miles.

"Look," Jessie said, pointing to a family of ducks. "The mother is leading her ducklings out on the lake to look for food."

"How old are they?" Benny asked.

"They may not be more than a day old," Aunt Jane answered. "Ducks can swim as soon as they are born."

"Really?" Benny said. He looked very impressed.

"Look at all those islands," Jessie said, pointing with her chin toward the small rocky islands in the middle of the lake.

"We won't go too much farther today," Henry called to the other canoe, when the group had been paddling for more than an hour.

"That's good," Benny cried. "I'm hungry!"

The forests began to thin into a clearing. In the distance, the Aldens could see the remains of an old wooden house. In front of the house was a field filled with blue, pink, and purple wildflowers.

"This might be a good campsite," Henry called to the others. "We could explore."

The Aldens and Aunt Jane paddled ashore and pulled the canoes out of the water. They tied the ropes around a trunk of a large pine tree and took out their backpacks, sleeping bags, and a small bag of food for dinner and breakfast.

A dirt road wound through the field and into a small pine forest. Aunt Jane suggested they set up camp near a stream under the pine trees.

"Somebody else also thought this would be a good campsite," Jessie said. She pointed to a heap of ashes on the ground.

"Henry and I will go back and get the tents out of the canoes," Aunt Jane said, putting her pack and sleeping bag on the ground.

"Benny, Violet, and I can gather wood for a campfire," Jessie suggested. "By the way, where is Benny?" she asked, as she turned around to look for her brother.

"He went to explore the old house in the clearing," Violet said. Both girls found Benny poking a pile of stones with a stick.

"This might have been a chimney once," Jessie said. The walls of the house had been made of wood, but now they lay in a pile of rubble.

"There's lots of wood here for a fire," Violet pointed out.

"Yes, let's gather some," Jessie said, stooping to pick up some wooden planks. "Watch out for the poison ivy," she warned her brother and sister. A thick patch grew alongside the house.

"I saw it. Henry showed me what it looked like in a book," Benny said proudly. "I didn't go near it."

Violet went into the forest near the house to gather smaller sticks and twigs.

She came running back to her brother and sister with a pile of sticks in her arms. "Come see what I've found!" she called to them.

Jessie and Benny followed her into the woods and stopped before a very large rock. Someone had painted a message on it.

"Look, there's writing on it!" Benny leaned forward to see better.

"Yes," Jessie agreed. "It looks like a riddle."

In a clear voice, Violet read:

> *"Silver and gold coins, so well hidden*
> *To seek and find them, you are bidden.*
> *A cat with whiskers but no feet*
> *Guards them near his silver sheet."*

"What does 'bidden' mean?" Benny looked at his sisters.

"It means telling someone to do something," Jessie answered.

"Oh," Benny said. "So, whoever wrote this message is telling us how to find a hidden treasure." Benny beamed.

His sisters smiled back at him.

"You know, Grandfather was wrong," Benny said. "We *have* found a mystery on the canoe trail."

CHAPTER 3

Night Noises

Jessie, Violet, and Benny rushed back to their campsite. Henry and Aunt Jane had already put up the tents. Aunt Jane was washing her hands in the stream.

"We'll have the hot dogs tonight," she said, reaching into the bag of food.

For once Benny wasn't interested in talking about food. "Aunt Jane, we found a riddle written on a rock near the old house," he almost shouted.

"A riddle?" Aunt Jane said.

"Really?" Henry asked. "What did it say?"

Jessie and Violet remembered it word for word and were able to repeat it.

"Can you show me where it is?" Henry asked.

"Maybe we should wait until after dinner," Jessie suggested.

"I am hungry," Benny admitted.

"So am I," Aunt Jane said.

"Why don't we wait," Violet told Henry. "It will still be light after dinner."

"Yes, and then we can look for more clues," Jessie added.

Henry and Jessie built the campfire.

Aunt Jane explored the campsite. "Lots of people must camp here. Look at the remains of all these campfires." She pointed to several piles of ashes on the ground.

"Yes, it's funny we haven't met any other canoeists so far," Jessie said. She pulled a large worn blanket from her backpack.

"This reminds me of when we lived in the boxcar," Benny said, as he helped Jessie gather a big pile of pine needles to put under the blanket. Violet picked some wildflowers.

"Things should look special for our first

meal on the trail," she said. She put the flowers in her tin cup and placed them in the middle of the picnic blanket.

Jessie took five plates, cups, forks, and spoons out of the bag of cooking utensils and set them on the blanket. Aunt Jane wrapped five potatoes in aluminum foil to put on the coals. Benny helped Henry punch holes in the hot dogs with a fork. Violet cut up some of Mrs. McGregor's fresh homemade bread for buns.

Soon dinner was ready and everything was delicious. They finished a loaf of Mrs. McGregor's homemade bread, ate up all the hot dogs and potatoes, and drank lots of water from the stream. Then they had fresh fruit and homemade brownies for dessert.

After dinner, Jessie boiled a big kettle of water and they all helped wash and dry the dishes. When everything had been put away, they walked to the big rock in the woods.

"Every word in a riddle means something," Aunt Jane said as she looked at the riddle on the rock.

"Silver and gold coins, so well hidden
To seek and find them, you are bidden.
A cat with whiskers but no feet
Guards them near his silver sheet."

"I wonder if they're talking about those coins that were stolen," Henry said.

"Could be," said Aunt Jane.

"Somewhere in this riddle is the clue to where the coins are hidden," said Jessie.

"They're 'well hidden,' " Henry said. "That doesn't tell us much of anything."

"You don't know," Aunt Jane answered. "Remember, every word in a riddle tries to tell you something."

"What do you think they mean by a cat with whiskers but no feet?" Benny asked. He looked a little discouraged.

"Wait a minute," Henry said. He had just thought of something. "Maybe they're talking about a place. Think of a place near here with the word *cat* in it." Henry looked teasingly at his brother.

"Catfish Lake!" Violet and Benny said at the same time.

"Good," Aunt Jane said. "Catfish certainly have whiskers but no feet."

"The silver sheet is the lake," Jessie said. "You know — when the water is calm it looks like a smooth silver sheet."

"Now we know the coins are hidden — well hidden — near Catfish Lake," Henry said.

"When will we be on Catfish Lake?" Benny asked.

"In a couple of days, at most," Henry answered.

"I think we've solved the riddle," Benny said.

"But we haven't found the coins yet," Henry said, laughing.

"Maybe there are more clues near the abandoned house," Violet suggested.

Aunt Jane and the Aldens searched the grounds around the house until it became dark. They found more piles of ashes in the woods.

"Someone sure is doing a lot of burning," Violet said.

"Yes, it might be campers making fires," Aunt Jane said.

"Or maybe only one person is making all these fires," Henry said.

"Maybe he or she is trying to burn any clues that might lead us to the coins," Jessie added.

Aunt Jane and the children nodded. It seemed there was nothing to do but go back to their campsite.

That night, all the Aldens fell asleep right away. Around midnight, Benny stirred. He thought he heard a sound.

Owowowowooooo . . . owowowooooo. . . .

Benny blinked and sat up in his sleeping bag. "Did you hear that?" he asked Henry.

But Henry was still sound asleep. It was very dark in the tent. Staying in his sleeping bag, Benny rolled across the floor until he could touch Henry's back.

"Henry," Benny whispered loudly. "Wake up! I think I hear a wolf outside the tent."

"Wolf," Henry muttered in his sleep.

Then Benny heard the sound again, only this time it was louder.

Owowowooooo . . . owowowooooo. . . .

This time Henry woke up. "Did you hear that wolf?" Benny asked.

"It sounds very far away," Henry said. "Try to go back to sleep, Benny. I'll stay awake for a little while and keep watch. Still, there are no wolves in this part of the country anymore. I'm sure there aren't." But not even Henry sounded so sure anymore.

CHAPTER 4

More Warnings

The next morning, the Aldens all slept until the sun was high in the sky. "It must be nearly nine o'clock," Henry said sleepily at breakfast.

"It took me a long time to fall back to sleep after hearing that wolf," Benny said.

Henry told the others about the sound they'd heard.

"It might have been a big dog," Violet said. "Wolves sound a bit like dogs." Violet loved animals and was always reading about them.

"Well, maybe it was a dog," Benny said. But he still looked worried.

"Well, at least your appetite didn't suffer, Benny." Aunt Jane smiled at her younger nephew.

Benny sat on the picnic blanket eating dried fruit and two large slices of Mrs. McGregor's homemade wheat bread.

"We'll probably finish all the homemade bread by tomorrow," Jessie said. "After that, we'll be having oatmeal for breakfast."

"I love oatmeal," Benny said. Suddenly he heard a rustling sound behind him.

"Did you hear that?" He tapped Henry on the arm.

A tall man with blue eyes and a black beard walked out of the woods toward them.

Aunt Jane stood up. "I'm Jane Bean," she said to the man, and introduced him to her nieces and nephews.

"I'm Lorenzo Espinosa." The man spoke softly. "Are those your canoes over there on the shore?"

"Yes," Henry answered. "We're taking a trip across Timberwolf Lake."

"How long have you been camping here?"

"Since last night," Jessie answered.

"How has your trip been so far?" Lorenzo looked at them closely. Violet thought he seemed suspicious about something.

"Fine, except for the wolf," Benny told him.

Lorenzo looked more worried than surprised. "I'm a scientist," he explained to Benny. "I study the plants and animals in these woods. There are no wolves around here."

"See, Benny, what did we tell you?" Henry said. "There's nothing to worry about."

"But, if I were you, I *would* worry," Lorenzo said, raising his voice, "not about wolves, but about. . . ." He paused. "Some very strange things have been going on near Timberwolf Lake," he finally continued.

"What kinds of things?" Aunt Jane asked.

"Well, I also heard your so-called wolf last night," Lorenzo said.

Benny sat up straighter and stopped eating.

"Don't worry. I'm sure it wasn't really a wolf," Lorenzo told Benny. "But I've heard this animal for the past week or so, on and off. I've also seen campfires burning at all hours."

"Don't campers usually make fires?" Aunt Jane asked.

"Yes, but you're the only campers I've seen all season, and you've only just arrived," Lorenzo said.

"Maybe someone is camping here in secret?" Henry suggested. "Maybe someone is trying to keep people off this lake on purpose," he continued.

"I don't know what to think!" Lorenzo exclaimed. "I've been coming up here every spring for the past fifteen years, and nothing like this has ever happened before."

For a few moments, Lorenzo did nothing but stare at the ground and scuff dirt over a little pile of pine needles. The Aldens just stared at him and didn't say a word.

"If I were you," Lorenzo continued, "I would go back. Don't try to get to the end of Timberwolf Lake. It's not safe. Too many strange things are happening."

The children looked at one another. Why was everyone trying to warn them away from the lake?

"We don't want to go home yet," Benny said. "We have to solve the riddle first."

"Do you know about the riddle written on the boulder?" Violet asked Lorenzo.

Lorenzo took a long time to answer. The children thought he seemed upset.

"I have more important things to worry about up here than a riddle," he said abruptly. "And so do you. You have to worry about storms this time of year, not to mention all this funny business."

Henry and Jessie exchanged glances. "We'll be very careful," Henry said.

"We really can't turn back now," Jessie told Lorenzo firmly. "Our grandfather is waiting to meet us at the end of the trail in White Pine."

"Well, you must do what you have to do," Lorenzo said. "But don't say I didn't warn you."

"We'll be careful," Violet told him. Again

there was a long pause before Lorenzo responded.

"You must excuse me," he finally said. "I have to go back to my cabin to check on my oak specimens." He suddenly seemed eager to get away from the Aldens.

"He wasn't very friendly," Jessie said a few minutes after Lorenzo had left.

"He might just be shy," Violet answered as she gathered up the dishes.

"He seemed kind of nervous when we asked him about the riddle," Henry said. He was helping Aunt Jane and Jessie take down the tents.

"I don't know what to think." Jessie shook her head. "Maybe he does know more than he wants to tell us."

"It's hard to know who we can trust on this trip so far," Henry remarked. "Maybe there *is* something strange on this lake. We could go another way and still meet Grandfather in White Pine."

"I don't think we need to change our plans yet," Aunt Jane said.

"Perhaps we shouldn't tell anyone else about the riddle until we find out more about it," Jessie suggested.

"We might find more clues when we get back on the lake," Violet said hopefully. "We shouldn't let those people talk us out of our canoe trip."

"Don't worry, Violet. We're going ahead." Henry smiled at his usually quiet sister.

An hour later Aunt Jane and the Aldens were canoeing toward one of the rocky islands in the middle of Timberwolf Lake. Puffy white clouds dotted the blue sky.

"I don't know why everyone is warning us about the weather," Henry said. "No sign of rain or storms today."

"Could we picnic on that rock island?" Benny asked. Today he sat in Henry's canoe with Violet.

"I don't see why not," Henry answered. "By the time we get there, it should be lunchtime."

When the Aldens paddled closer to the island, they saw it was just a very large gray boulder. Small pine trees and vines grew from its cracks.

Henry and Aunt Jane tied the canoes around a tree trunk and clambered up the boulder in their sneakers. Jessie put bread, dried fruit, and cheddar cheese in a small backpack to take with them. Violet took her sketch pad, and Benny grabbed his softball.

"Look, we're scaring away the geese and loons," Benny said, as he ran to where Henry and Aunt Jane were standing.

"Yes, they'll have to find a new place to sun themselves for now," Aunt Jane said.

"I'm sure they'll be back when we start eating," Henry said.

Benny ran all around the rock island before coming back to see what was in Jessie's pack for lunch.

Violet explored more slowly. She touched the pine trees and tall rushes that grew in the nooks and crannies of the rocks. For a long time, she stared out in the distance at a pair of jagged rocks further down the lake.

"I'm looking for a good scene to draw," Violet announced at lunch.

"Can't you draw us eating?" Benny asked after taking a big bite of his cheese sandwich.

"Well, I could," Violet said. "But I thought I would draw those jagged rocks over there." She pointed across the lake. "You know, it looks as though there might be something written on them."

"Goodness, you're right," Aunt Jane said, shading her eyes to see better.

Jessie, Henry, and Benny looked too. They saw some faint reddish brown letters painted on the rocks.

"We're too far away to read what those letters say. Maybe we could canoe closer to the rocks right after lunch," Jessie said.

"I don't think we should try to push ourselves too hard today," Aunt Jane said. "We had a long day yesterday."

"I agree," Henry said. "Let's just relax on our own private island. We can go see those rocks later this afternoon. They're on the way to our next campsite."

The Aldens and Aunt Jane finished the last of their picnic lunch. After they had cleaned up, Violet got her sketch pad and drew.

Henry read his book of Sherlock Holmes mystery stories. Jessie and Benny tossed the ball back and forth with Aunt Jane.

It was mid-afternoon when Aunt Jane and the Aldens got back in their canoes. They soon reached the jagged rocks.

"Hold the canoe steady," Henry said to Violet, who sat behind him paddling. She stopped and planted her paddle in the water.

Henry adjusted his binoculars and looked through them for a long time. Or at least it seemed long to the others.

"Can you read it?" Jessie finally asked from the other canoe. She had pulled her boat very close to Henry's.

"I think it says KEEP OUT," Henry answered, still looking through the binoculars. "Someone wrote that sign with red spray paint."

"May I take a look?" Violet asked.

Henry handed her the binoculars.

"Yes, it definitely says, KEEP OUT," Violet said. "There's also a drawing of a skull and crossbones near the sign."

"Do you think it means keep off the rocks, or off the lake?" Benny asked.

"It could mean the rocks," Henry said. "But I have a feeling, it means stay off the lake."

"Well, that's our third warning since we left," Aunt Jane said grimly. No one could argue.

CHAPTER 5

A Stranger

The Aldens passed the jagged gray rocks and kept paddling. After two hours, they reached the narrow strip of land that separated Timberwolf from Catfish Lake.

"We're going to have to carry the canoes for a little way," Henry said.

"Is this what they call a portage?" Violet asked, pointing to the trail between the two lakes.

"Yes, it's like a walking path," Henry explained.

Carefully, Henry and Aunt Jane pulled their canoes up the shore of Timberwolf Lake. Henry took the tents, sleeping bags, and waterproof bags out of the canoes. Jessie strapped the paddles inside them.

Together, Henry and Jessie lifted the front of one canoe. With Jessie's help, Henry swung the canoe up over his head and then walked the short distance to Catfish Lake.

Jessie helped Aunt Jane carry the other canoe. Benny and Violet followed, carrying one of the tents between them. Once Henry and Aunt Jane had secured the canoes at the edge of Catfish Lake, they went back to get the rest of the equipment.

"Our campsite should be at the end of this path," Henry said, looking at the map. The others were busy repacking the canoes with all the gear.

"I think that might be the trail," Aunt Jane said. She pointed to a dirt road that veered away from the walking path.

"Let's follow it," Henry said, shouldering his backpack. The others took their packs and Jessie brought another small bag of food.

"Let's leave the tents in the canoes for now," Henry said. "I think there may be cabins at this campsite."

Thick oak trees grew on each side of the path. Their leafy branches met in mid-air, shading the trail. Aunt Jane and the Aldens had not gone far when they spied a canoe hidden in the underbrush.

"Look, another canoe!" Benny sounded very excited. "Do you think it belongs to Lorenzo?"

"I don't know." Henry seemed doubtful. "We're a bit far from Lorenzo's cabin."

"That's good," Benny said. "He scared me a little. What if he's one of the coin burglars?"

"Oh, Benny," Violet said, "we have no proof of that."

"Well, he did act pretty nervous," Benny reminded her.

At a bend in the trail, the Aldens saw a wooden lean-to.

"We get to sleep in a house tonight," Benny said, skipping toward it.

"I smell something cooking." Jessica

sniffed the air. "There may be other canoeists here."

No sooner had Jessie spoken than a red-haired man limped over to them from behind the lean-to. The man wore a green flannel shirt, blue jeans, and only one sneaker. His other foot was bound up in a towel.

"Did you hurt your foot?" Benny blurted out.

"Yes," the camper said. "I twisted my ankle in a large hole outside the lean-to this morning. The strange thing is I never noticed the hole there before." The man spoke in a clipped British accent.

Aunt Jane and the Aldens looked at each other. They were not the only ones noticing mysterious things on the canoe trail.

"Is that your canoe back there on the trail?" Jessie asked.

"And is that your food we smell cooking?" Benny asked before the man could answer.

"Yes to both questions," the man replied, laughing a little. He introduced himself as Rob Wilson.

"I had to leave my canoe on the path be-

cause I couldn't carry it with my twisted ankle," Rob explained.

"We could move it to the lake for you," Henry suggested.

"Thank you," Rob said. "That would be very helpful. I was planning on canoeing down Catfish Lake, but now I'm not too sure of my plans. I may stay at this campsite a while longer until my ankle gets better."

"I don't know how you can manage." Aunt Jane shook her head. "It's hard enough to canoe alone without a twisted ankle."

"Yes, nothing's gone right since the beginning of my trip," Rob confided.

"What do you mean?" Henry asked right away.

"Well, the sprained ankle was the main thing." He suddenly grew quiet, almost as if he were afraid he'd said too much.

"Are you on vacation?" Benny asked him.

"Not exactly," Rob answered.

Jessie noticed he wanted to change the subject. "Have you been on this trail long?" she asked.

"No, only two days," he said in his clipped

speech. Suddenly he turned away.

"Oh, please excuse me. I must take my fish off the grill," he said quickly. After removing the fish, he packed his food in a basket, and limped into the woods.

"Where is he going with all that food?" Benny wondered.

"Shhh, Benny. He might hear you," Violet said. "Maybe he just wants to eat in peace."

Aunt Jane and the Aldens ate their macaroni and cheese dinner outside the lean-to, which they would be sharing with Rob Wilson. "Do you think we scared him away by asking him all those questions?" Jessie asked.

"It's hard to tell," Aunt Jane said. "He did seem friendlier at first — before we asked him about his trip."

"Everyone we've met seems to have something to hide," Henry observed, thinking of Lorenzo Espinosa and now Rob Wilson.

"Well, at least Rob Wilson isn't warning us to stay away from this lake, like everyone else is," Violet pointed out.

"Yes, he's even going in the same direction

we are," Jessie said. "He must not think Timberwolf Lake and Catfish Lake are dangerous."

"Do you think he's trying to solve the riddle, too?" Benny asked.

"I don't know," Henry said. "We really don't know anything about him yet. I don't think we should tell him too much."

"Can't we tell him about the riddle or the coin robberies?" Benny wanted to know.

"No, I think we should first find out why he's on this trail." Henry sounded firm.

"Henry, it's not like you to be suspicious of everyone," Aunt Jane remarked. "But I agree, it's best to be careful."

Rob had not returned by the time the Aldens were ready to go to sleep.

"I hope he doesn't snore," Benny said. He lay inside his sleeping bag on the bottom bunk. Henry was in the top bunk reading his book by the light of his flashlight.

"That's the least of our worries, Benny," Henry said.

Benny gulped. "Do you think Rob Wilson is a burglar?" He motioned across the room to Rob's empty bunk. Rob had left a large backpack and two fishing poles on top of his sleeping bag.

"I don't know what to think about Rob. But he's probably all right." Henry tried to sound comforting.

"I hope we won't hear any wild animals tonight," Benny said sleepily.

"I hope not, Benny," Henry said softly. He looked down and saw Benny's eyes were closed. It never took Benny very long to fall asleep, no matter where he was.

CHAPTER 6

The Storm

Nothing unusual happened that night. Everyone slept very well, even Rob Wilson, who must have returned very late. He came limping out of the lean-to in the middle of the Alden's breakfast.

"May I join you?" Rob asked. They nodded, and he sat down beside Jessie. Although he still limped, he said the swelling on his ankle had gone down.

"This is the first good night's sleep I've gotten since my canoe trip began," he confided. He poured some orange juice from his thermos and offered some to the Aldens. They shook their heads.

They were drinking the hot chocolate Jessie had made. It was cold in the mornings, and the air smelled of pine and wood smoke.

They had woken up early to prepare breakfast — hot oatmeal with lots of brown sugar and raisins. Rob reached in his pack and pulled out a loaf of hard bread. He broke off a piece for himself and hungrily eyed the Alden's big pot of oatmeal.

"Would you like some?" Violet offered, passing him a bowl.

"Thank you. I'll only take a little," Rob said. He ate his portion quickly. "It's wonderful," he said between mouthfuls. "You must let me cook a meal for you before you leave this campsite."

Aunt Jane and the Aldens looked at each other. Henry still could not decide whether or not to trust Rob. No one said much to him at breakfast. They were all too busy eating.

"He does seem much friendlier today," Jessie remarked softly after Rob left to get his binoculars from the cabin. He wanted to do some bird-watching.

"Well, having a good night's sleep helps," Aunt Jane said. "He seems much more relaxed than he did yesterday."

When Rob came out of the cabin, Benny was eating a second bowl of oatmeal.

"So you're still hungry," Rob teased, poking Benny playfully in the ribs. Henry and Jessie exchanged glances. Why was Rob so friendly today and so quiet and secretive yesterday?

The Aldens decided to stay another night at their comfortable campsite. They wanted to do some fishing and get to know Rob better.

"I just wish he would tell us more about his canoe trip," Henry said. "What did he mean when he said nothing had gone right since he got on this trail?"

"Well, we're not telling him too much ourselves," Violet reminded her brother.

"That's true. Maybe he doesn't want to trust anyone, either," Henry commented.

"Oh, you'll probably win him over in time," Aunt Jane said.

She was right. In the afternoon, Rob took Jessie and Henry fishing and helped them catch enough trout for dinner.

By the end of the day, the Aldens had learned how to bone and clean fish. But they were still no closer to knowing more about Rob, or his reasons for being on the canoe trail.

"I think we should invite him to come with us," Jessie said at dinner. She leaned over her plate and took a bite of her fish.

Jessie, Violet, Benny, and Aunt Jane were all enjoying fresh trout, rice, and a lentil salad Aunt Jane had prepared. She always ate healthy foods. Rob was with Henry, cooking the rest of the fish over the coals.

"Now that we know him better, that's a good idea," Aunt Jane agreed. "It would be hard for him to finish his trip alone with a swollen ankle."

"He wouldn't be able to push his canoe up to the shore by himself," Violet said.

"Or push it out onto the lake," Benny added.

The next morning, Aunt Jane, the Aldens, and Rob Wilson were up early. Rob was delighted to join the others for the rest of their trip. He was able to pack most of the gear he needed in Henry and Violet's canoe. The Alden children moved the rest of his belongings to the woods for safekeeping.

The sky was streaked with pinkish gray clouds when Henry pushed the canoes out onto the water. "It's overcast today," he observed.

Jessie looked at the sky before plunging her paddle into the water. She steered her canoe until she was alongside Henry's. The air felt very still.

As they softly paddled their canoes in the calm water, they spotted wood ducks, meadowlarks, and two bald eagles.

The eagles flew overhead together. With their wings spread, they were much larger than Benny. He stared at them, open-mouthed.

All the animals seemed nervous. The ducklings swam around their mothers. The geese honked. The meadowlarks twittered and flew around in circles.

"There might be a rainstorm coming," Violet observed. "That could be why the animals are acting that way."

"It may not be too bad a storm," Rob said, glancing at the sky. "If it were serious, the animals wouldn't be out at all. They would find shelter."

Fog began to move in slowly. Henry noticed it was getting a little harder to see the shoreline. Violet watched the tops of trees disappear into a haze. To Aunt Jane, it seemed as if the water became grayer and grayer.

"It's getting windy," Henry said to his crew. Small waves lapped against the canoe. Then suddenly the fog blew in with much more force. Soon everything was covered in a thick gray mist.

"Maybe we should paddle ashore and wait until this fog lifts," Henry suggested to Rob and Violet. Even though they were sitting in his canoe, he could barely see them. He couldn't see the shoreline at all. And worst of all, he could not find Aunt Jane's canoe, which had been close beside his only a moment ago.

"Jessie, Aunt Jane, Benny! Can you hear us?" Henry and Violet called. There was no answer. Rob cupped his hands and shouted, too. But their voices were drowned out by the sound of rain hitting the water.

Luckily, it was a light rain, more like a drizzle. But it combined with the wind, which churned the water and shook the trees.

Henry and Violet paddled in a big circle to see if they could find the others. They called and called into the fog. But there was never any answer. Aunt Jane's canoe had vanished!

CHAPTER 7

Angela Comes Back

When the fog blew in, Aunt Jane and Jessie decided to paddle ashore. They thought Henry's canoe was right behind them, but it wasn't.

Jessie and Benny called very loudly to let Henry and Violet know where they were. But their voices were carried away by the wind. There was no response.

It was hard to see where the shore was. Very slowly, Aunt Jane and Jessie were able to steer themselves to the nearest bank.

As they pulled the canoe out of the water,

the wind grew stronger. The waves became larger and splattered over the edge of the canoe.

"We got out of the water just in time," Jessie said.

She tied the canoe's rope around the trunk of a tree and brushed her wet hair out of her eyes. Then she quickly rummaged through the backpacks for the rain jackets. She handed Benny the bright red one. Hers was her favorite color, a rich royal blue. It made her feel better just to put it on.

"I certainly hope the others are all right," Aunt Jane said. She looked very worried as she pulled on her pale green rain jacket.

"I thought they were right behind us," Jessie said. She looked toward the lake but could only see a few feet in front of her.

"Henry is an experienced canoeist. I'm sure he'll steer them ashore safely." Aunt Jane sounded as if she was trying to convince herself.

"And Rob Wilson is with them. He'll know what to do," Jessie pointed out.

The fog grew thicker and thicker. Soon

Jessie could barely see her hands when she held them in front of her. She huddled near Benny and Aunt Jane under the pine trees.

"It's lucky there's no thunder or lightning," Aunt Jane commented.

"That's good," Benny said. He held out his hand to Jessie. When he realized she couldn't see it, he tapped her arm.

Jessie grabbed his hand and squeezed it. "Don't worry, Benny. We'll be all right. It's not a bad storm."

"No, but it's very bad fog." Aunt Jane groped in front of her until she found Jessie's arm. She gave it a gentle pat. Above them, the pine and oak trees swayed in the wind.

The water came farther and farther up onto the shore. It swirled around the canoe and gently rocked it from side to side. Aunt Jane suggested that they move up the bank.

"You know, Henry and Violet probably paddled ashore, too. We just can't see them from where we are," Benny said.

"I hope so," Jessie replied.

Half an hour later, the fog began to lift a little. Aunt Jane and the Aldens were surprised to see another canoe tied up not far from theirs.

"I bet that's Henry's canoe!" Benny shouted, running toward it.

"I don't think so," Jessie said.

"That's a wooden canoe. Henry's is made of aluminum," Aunt Jane pointed out.

Jessie grabbed a plastic pail from their canoe and began to bail it out. Aunt Jane and Benny looked in the bag of food for something to eat. They did not notice two men coming up behind them.

"So, you got caught in the storm, too," one of the men said.

Aunt Jane jumped. Jessie dropped her pail of water.

The two men were very tall. One had long blond hair. The other had short, wavy dark hair. Both men looked as if they hadn't shaved in a few days. Their clothes were very rumpled.

"Sorry, we didn't mean to scare you," the blond man said. He had a loud, booming voice.

The other man sneezed loudly and groped

in his pockets for a handkerchief.

The men introduced themselves as Matt and Bill. Matt was the blond one. They told Aunt Jane, Benny, and Jessie they worked for the forestry service.

"We're mapping some canoe routes," Matt explained. "This old canoe has gotten us around very well." He pointed to his wooden one. "We had to come ashore when the fog rolled in."

Jessie told Matt and Bill about getting separated from the rest of their party.

"I wouldn't worry," Matt said. "If your brother is an experienced canoeist, he should have been all right in this storm."

"Luckily, we went over our camping plans before we got separated," Aunt Jane said. "I think they probably went right on to the next campsite when the fog began to lift. We can find them tomorrow."

"Where are you headed?" Matt asked. He seemed to do more talking than Bill.

"Down Catfish Lake toward White Pine," Aunt Jane answered.

"Have you run into many people on these trails?" Matt asked.

"No, not too many," Aunt Jane said. Matt asked several more questions, but Aunt Jane's answers were brief. She gave Jessie and Benny a warning look. With all the odd things that had been happening, they had agreed not to give strangers too much information.

"But they're forest rangers," Jessie whispered when the two men had gone. After inviting the others to join them for dinner, Matt and Bill had left to get some food from their tent.

"Yes, I know," Aunt Jane said. "But they asked a lot of questions. I don't see why they wanted to know so much about us."

"They were very curious," Jessie admitted. "But maybe they need to keep track of how many tourists are using these trails."

"Well, yes, I did think of that." Aunt Jane sounded doubtful. "Still, you never know." Her voice trailed off as she heard Matt and Bill approach.

"Can't we at least tell them about the wolf calls?" Benny whispered to Jessie. Jessie nodded.

Matt and Bill brought canned spaghetti and a bag of marshmallows with them. The Aldens supplied juice, coffee, and some of Aunt Jane's lentil salad.

Matt and Bill seemed delighted when Jessie offered to build the campfire. Benny found sticks to roast marshmallows.

"Delicious," Aunt Jane said later when she took a bite of spaghetti and tomato sauce. Anything would have tasted good to her after the storm.

"Listen, we don't mean to scare you," Bill began. He toyed with his spaghetti. "But we were wondering if anything unusual had happened to you on your trip so far," Bill continued.

"We thought we heard a wolf," Benny said. He told the two forest rangers all about their first night on the trail, but he did not mention the riddle.

Jessie, after a nod from Aunt Jane, told them about meeting Lorenzo Espinosa and

Rob Wilson, and about the warnings they had received. Matt and Bill listened closely.

"I'm glad you're telling us all this," Matt said. He stirred his coffee and cleared his throat. "You haven't met a woman on this trail, a well-dressed woman with long blonde hair?"

Aunt Jane, Jessie, and Benny all looked at one another. "No, not on the trail," Jessie answered. "But that does sound like someone we saw in the store where we rented our canoes."

"I don't think this woman would be renting a canoe," Matt said. He reached for a stick and started toasting a marshmallow over the coals.

"Oh, she wasn't renting. She wanted a map," Jessie explained.

Matt and Bill looked at one another and did not ask any more questions. Benny put a fresh marshmallow on his stick and went to sit by Matt.

"You know, I've never met a forest ranger before," he told Matt. "How come you aren't in a uniform?"

Matt turned and smiled at Benny. "Oh, we don't wear them this early in the season. We'll wear them when more tourists start coming."

"What color are your uniforms?" Benny asked.

"Green," Matt answered abruptly.

"Brown," Bill said at the same time.

Then Bill laughed, but he sounded nervous. "It depends on the season," he explained.

"Oh, look, my marshmallow is burning!" Matt yelled. He blew on the stick until the flame went out. As he pulled the burnt gooey marshmallow off his stick, it stuck to his fingers.

"Ouch!" he yelled. "It's burning me!" He got up and waved his hand up and down.

Jessie rushed to get the first-aid kit.

"You should probably put your hand in cold water right away," Aunt Jane suggested kindly. She pointed to the lake.

After Matt had soaked his finger in the lake, Jessie found ointment and a gauze bandage to put on the burn. "There," she said,

as she finished taping up Matt's finger. "It should be all right now."

"Thank you," Matt said a little sheepishly. "We didn't bring any first-aid equipment with us."

Bill suddenly gave Matt a warning glance and put his fingers to his lips. Jessie was busy putting away the first-aid kit. Benny and Aunt Jane were putting up their tent. No one saw Matt and Bill signal one another.

"Good luck on the rest of your trip," Matt called. "We're going back to our tent now. We need a good night's rest."

"Yes, and we hope you meet up with the rest of your family tomorrow," Bill added. They left the campfire for the Aldens.

"Do you think they really work for the forestry service?" Jessie asked as she laid the sleeping bags inside the tent.

"I don't know," Aunt Jane answered. "But I must say, they didn't seem to know too much about campfires or treating burns."

"They may just have been tired from the storm," Jessie said. She rummaged in her backpack for her red wool socks. It got much colder in the evenings.

"Maybe." Aunt Jane sounded doubtful. "But I had a funny feeling about them. They didn't seem as if they were used to the outdoors."

"You mean they may not really be forest rangers?" Benny sounded disappointed. He was busy unrolling his sleeping bag.

"They might be," Aunt Jane said. "But I'm not sure." She yawned and got into her sleeping bag. She was already sound asleep when Jessie tucked Benny into his.

In the middle of the night, Jessie stirred and was soon wide-awake. She heard something rustling outside. What if it's a bear? she thought to herself. Or maybe it's a raccoon. That thought was much more comforting.

Suddenly she saw a very bright light shining outside. At first she was frightened, but then she realized it was probably just Matt or Bill getting up in the middle of the night for some reason.

Just as suddenly as it had come on, the

light flickered and vanished. It took Jessie a long time to fall back to sleep.

Meanwhile, Henry, Violet, and Rob had given up trying to find the other canoe in the fog. They went ashore until the fog lifted. Then they decided to go to the next campsite.

Henry guided the canoe across the lake. Before long, Henry and Violet spotted a low building in the distance.

"I'm sure that's the bunkhouse," Henry said happily. He had been worried they would never find it in the storm. "Now, we can just wait here for the others."

"Are you sure Jessie and Aunt Jane know where this campsite is?" Violet asked.

"Yes, I pointed it out to them on the map," Henry answered. "And Jessie has her compass."

"They're probably waiting out the storm onshore somewhere," Rob suggested. He slowly limped toward the building they had seen from the water and disappeared inside.

Henry and Violet followed with some food and their backpacks.

"Oh, no," Henry suddenly said, more to himself than anyone else. Outside the bunkhouse was a wooden canoe with the name *Angela* carved in big red letters on both sides.

"It can't be the same Angela we met in the store," Violet said. "She had nothing good to say about this canoe trail."

"I hope you're right," Henry said grimly, opening the door to the bunkhouse.

Violet looked around and smiled. The bunkhouse had a fireplace in the main room. A soft rug covered the wooden floor. All the bedrooms had wooden bunk beds built into the walls.

"It will be fun to wait for the others in a place like this." Violet adjusted her purple hair ribbon.

"Yes," Henry agreed. "It is a nice bunkhouse."

"Well, I thought I'd have the place to myself this evening," a familiar voice interrupted.

"Angela," Henry said. "We thought you didn't like to canoe on this lake."

Angela had just entered. She wore fancy waterproof shorts, gold jewelry, and a red sweater with white canoes all over it. Violet noticed the color of her watchband matched the red in her sweater.

"I had some business up here," Angela said, "or don't worry, I wouldn't be anywhere near this awful place." She put her enormous backpack on the ground with a thud.

Rob came out of one of the bedrooms to see who Violet and Henry were talking to. Violet thought he turned very pale when he saw Angela.

"Hello, I'm Rob Wilson." He held out his hand.

"You're staying here, too?" Angela asked rudely. She ignored his outstretched hand.

"I could ask you the same question," Rob answered.

Angela glared.

"Will you be staying here tonight?" Henry asked politely.

"Well, yes," Angela said. "In case you haven't noticed, it's a miserable night out."

She turned back to Rob. "So who are you?" she demanded.

"I'm a tourist," Rob answered.

"From England?" Angela asked.

"Yes." Rob looked more and more nervous.

"How would you have heard about Timberwolf Lake or Catfish Lake in England? This is a very isolated part of the country," Angela remarked.

"I live here now," Rob said. He seemed eager to end the conversation.

"You're all canoeing together?" Angela wanted to know.

"Yes," Violet said shyly. "We met Rob at a campsite a couple of days ago."

"They very kindly invited me to join them when they saw I'd twisted my ankle," Rob said with a grateful look at Henry and Violet.

Angela suddenly noticed there were fewer children. "Where's the rest of your family?"

"We got separated in the storm," Henry explained.

Rob cleared his throat. "So, what sort of business are you doing?" he asked Angela.

"I'd rather not talk about it," she snapped. "Now, if you'll excuse me, I must go rest." She struggled with her backpack and strode out of the room.

When Henry and Violet looked at Rob, he was staring down at the floor. He looked as if he'd just seen a ghost. Without a word, he went back to his room.

Henry and Violet changed out of their wet clothes and had some lunch. Then they walked down to the lake to see if they could spot Aunt Jane's canoe. Now that the fog had lifted, the lake shone in the late afternoon sun. A small rainbow appeared in the distance.

"What do you think is the matter with Rob?" Violet asked as they walked along the shore.

"I don't know." Henry sighed. "He seemed so nervous after seeing Angela."

"It's too bad he won't talk to us," Violet said.

"I really wish Angela wasn't at this campsite," Henry said. "There's something very suspicious about her. If the others were here, I'd move on."

He reached their canoe and bent down to see if it needed bailing. "Oh no!" he groaned.

"What's the matter?" Violet asked. She looked down at the canoe and gasped. Everything in it was gone, even the paddles!

CHAPTER 8

A Discovery

"Violet, look!" Henry called to his sister the next morning. "It's Aunt Jane's canoe!" Henry and Violet ran down to the lake. It was early, and the sky was a little pink.

"Henry, Violet, we found you!" Benny called. He tumbled out of the canoe when it reached shore. Henry held the canoe steady while Aunt Jane and Jessie climbed out.

"Oh, I'm so happy to see you," Aunt Jane exclaimed. She gave Violet and Henry a big hug. So did Jessie. Benny hopped up and down excitedly.

After they'd unloaded the canoe, the Aldens and Aunt Jane sat down on a log for a snack of graham crackers and peanut butter.

Henry and Violet told the others about their things being stolen.

"It was lucky we'd taken most of our food and clothes out of the canoe," Violet explained.

"You really think it was Angela who took everything?" Jessie asked.

"She was gone when we got back to the bunkhouse," Violet said.

"So was her canoe," Henry added. "She just disappeared."

Henry didn't say so, but he suspected Rob, too. Rob hadn't been in his room the night before, when Henry and Violet got back from their walk. Henry hadn't seen him all morning either.

"Well, at least we're all together and safe." Aunt Jane said, interrupting Henry's thoughts. She hugged Violet and Henry for perhaps the fourth time that morning. "I really was worried when we got separated," she admitted.

"I don't know how Angela did it," Violet said, still puzzled. She shook her head. "She had so many things with her already. She took our tent, our sleeping bags, our life jackets. . . ."

"I brought extra inflatable life preservers in my backpack," Jessie reminded her. "We'll be all right."

Henry agreed. "We don't have too much further to go," he said. "We can all sleep in one tent if we have to. Our big problem will be finding new paddles."

"Why don't we try to find some long poles in the woods?" Jessie suggested.

"That might work," Henry said, but he sounded doubtful. "Still, it would be hard to find just the right size and shape. Even if we did, it would be hard to grip rough wood for a very long time."

"We have two paddles in our canoe," Aunt Jane reminded him. "Just take one of ours. We can both manage with only one paddle."

Henry looked serious. "The only problem is we have some small rapids to cross just before White Pine. It might be hard to do that with only one person paddling."

"I think we'll be all right," Aunt Jane said. She was an excellent canoeist, and she knew Henry was very skilled as well.

"It looks like another storm is coming," Jessie remarked. "We might as well stay at this campsite another night and not try to cross rapids in this weather. We still have time before we're supposed to meet Grandfather."

"Good idea," Violet said. She stood up and wiped the cracker crumbs from her lavender shorts. "Besides, now that we're finally on Catfish Lake, we should be looking for clues to solve that riddle."

"That's what I was thinking," Benny said.

"Oh, my goodness, there's Rob," Aunt Jane said. "I'd forgotten all about him."

Rob slowly limped toward them from the bunkhouse. He looked very pale, and there were big dark circles under his eyes.

"It seems like his ankle is worse," Aunt Jane said softly.

"You're here!" Rob exclaimed to Aunt Jane, Jessie, and Benny as he came closer.

"Yes, we made it," Aunt Jane laughed. "It was lucky Henry and I planned our route before we left. I knew he would be heading to this campsite."

"Would you like some peanut butter and crackers?" Violet asked shyly.

Rob rubbed his eyes and sat down beside Aunt Jane. He looked very worried. "No, thank you. I think I'll just make myself some coffee. I'm not very hungry."

"Did you know we were robbed?" Henry asked him.

A little more color seemed to drain from Rob's face. "No, I had no idea," he said.

"They took everything we left in the canoe," Henry explained.

"Even the paddles," Benny added.

"Angela?" Rob asked.

"We're not sure." Henry looked closely at Rob. "But she's gone now."

"What a shame." Rob shook his head.

"We're staying here another night," Benny announced. "There are some things we want to look for in the woods."

Henry gave Benny a warning look, but

Rob didn't seem to notice.

"Okay," Rob said, but his thoughts seemed faraway. "I'll be in the bunkhouse if you need me. I need to catch up on some sleep."

As they walked through the woods in back of the bunkhouse, Jessie told Henry all about meeting Matt and Bill.

"They didn't act like forest rangers," Benny added.

Henry sighed. "I think we should sit down and talk about all this." He pointed to some big boulders under the trees. When they were all seated, he told Jessie, Benny, and Aunt Jane how mysterious Rob had been acting.

"He hasn't been himself since we ran into Angela," Violet added.

"That doesn't mean he took our stuff," Jessie said. She hated to think that Rob might be a thief.

"I can't prove he took anything." Henry sighed. "All I know is he wasn't in the bunkhouse all evening. After he met Angela, we didn't see him again until this morning."

"He didn't seem to like Angela any more than we did," Violet added.

"No, but I think he knows more than he's letting on," Henry remarked.

Jessie pulled a piece of paper and a pen out of her rain jacket. "I think we should make a list of all the people we suspect," she said.

"It seems like no one wants us on this trail," Violet said. "But I still think Angela is the most suspicious."

"I think so, too," Benny added.

"But," Henry said, "how would she have had time to take all our things, pack them away somewhere, and get away?"

"I'll put Angela on the list along with Lorenzo, Rob, Matt, and Bill," Jessie said. "All of them, except maybe Rob, have tried to talk us out of continuing our trip."

"Well, Matt and Bill didn't really try to stop us," Benny said.

"No," Jessie agreed. "But they seemed suspicious. They said they were forest rangers, but they didn't act like real rangers," Jessie reminded her brother. "And they asked a lot of questions."

"Do you think Lorenzo is really a scientist?" Benny asked.

"I don't know," Jessie answered. "There are certainly people on this trail pretending to be things they aren't." Jessie wrote *scientist* with a question mark next to Lorenzo's name.

"It's funny, everyone's acting so strange," Violet remarked. "What do they think we know?"

"Or what do they think we'll find out?" Henry said.

"Let's see." Jessie was still busy writing. "I believe Lorenzo was the only person we talked to about the riddle."

"That's right," Henry nodded. "And we didn't talk to anyone about the coin robberies."

"We won't know anything about the coins unless we look for some clues," Benny reminded his family. Everyone agreed. Benny ran on ahead and disappeared in a grove of pine trees.

Jessie put away her paper and chased after

him. "We don't really know what we're look-ing for," she said as they both stopped to catch their breath.

They were surrounded by pine and oak trees. The trees were so tall, they blocked out what little light there was that day.

Benny walked on ahead while Jessie waited for Violet to catch up.

"I wish it weren't so overcast," Violet commented when she reached her sister. "It makes this forest look very eerie."

"There's a big meadow up ahead," Benny said, running back to his sisters. "I also saw another old house."

"Really? Let's go see it," Jessie said. By then Henry and Aunt Jane had joined them. Together, they all walked quickly through the woods to the meadow.

The meadow around the house was large and overgrown. Clumps of buttercups and daisies grew near the house.

"Oh, look at all these beautiful flowers!" Violet said. Her eyes were shining.

"Oh, Violet, don't waste time picking

flowers. Come see the big old house." Benny took his sister's hand.

"Okay. Benny, I'm coming." Violet laughed and ran toward the house with her brother.

"Careful, those steps don't look too safe," Aunt Jane warned Benny and Violet.

The house was built of wood and painted a faded mustard yellow. It had white shutters and a porch that sagged. The porch steps were broken and so were many of the windowpanes.

"This house must be about one hundred years old," Henry said.

Benny climbed onto the porch. "I don't think anyone lives here," he said.

"No, it looks abandoned," Henry agreed.

Benny pulled on the ornate doorknob. "It's locked," he reported. He tugged some more, but soon gave up and went around to the back.

"Hey!" he called to the others. "I've found something else!"

They found Benny standing by an old

stone well near the back of the house.

"That's an old well, Benny," Henry said. "It must belong to the house. It was probably built before there was running water."

"That's it!" Violet's eyes were shining. The others looked puzzled.

"What's it?" Henry asked.

"Remember the riddle?" Violet asked. Jessie smiled and pulled a piece of paper out of her big pocket.

" 'Silver and gold coins, so well hidden,' " she read.

"Of course," Henry smiled. "The coins are hidden *in a well*!"

"And we are near Catfish Lake," Jessie reminded them all.

Henry leaned over the edge of the well.

"Can you see anything?" Benny asked a bit impatiently.

"Be careful," Aunt Jane warned Henry.

"Don't worry, Aunt Jane," Henry said. He was leaning so far into the well, his voice sounded muffled.

"Well, do you see anything?" Benny repeated.

"No," Henry answered. "Maybe I should go back for my flashlight."

"I have an idea," Jessie said. "Why don't we first see if any of these stones are loose?" She began prying the stones on the top.

Henry, Violet, Benny, and Aunt Jane set to work helping her. To Benny it seemed as if more than an hour had gone by before Violet shouted, "I found a loose stone."

The others crowded around her. The loose stone was three rows down from the top of the wall.

"Careful," Henry warned. "You don't want all the stones around it to fall out, too."

"This is the only stone that's loose," Jessie pointed out.

Slowly, Jessie and Violet wiggled and pried the stone until it came out from the wall of the well.

"Is there anything behind it?" Benny asked.

"Yes, I see something," Jessie reported excitedly. She reached in the hole and slowly pulled out a brown leather pouch.

"Wow, it's really heavy," she said as she

dropped it onto the ground.

They all sat in the long grass by the well and watched Benny unbuckle the pouch. Inside were almost one hundred gold and silver coins.

"Oh, some of these coins are so pretty," Violet exclaimed. She held up a silver coin with an oak tree engraved on it. "This one is dated 1652." She laid the coin on a rock.

"Most of them seem to be early American colonial coins," Aunt Jane said. She fingered a large gold piece from the 1700s with an eagle on it.

"Look at this one!" Henry almost shouted. He held up a heavy gold coin. It had an engraving of a sunrise coming up over mountains on one side. On the back was an eagle with a shield and the date — 1787.

"Do you know what that is?" A familiar voice spoke behind them. Without waiting for an answer, the voice continued. "It's a famous gold doubloon. Some collectors would do anything to get their hands on it."

The Aldens turned to find Rob staring at the coins laid out on the rock.

CHAPTER 9

Rob's Story

"I guess I owe you an explanation," Rob said. He put his walking stick down and sat by the Aldens in the long grass.

"You've just found one of the most valuable private collections of early American coins in the country," he continued.

"Was it stolen about a year ago?" Henry asked, remembering the conversation in the pizzeria.

"Yes." Rob nodded. "From Mr. Orville Withington. He hired me as a private detective to try to find it."

"So you're not a burglar?" Benny sounded very relieved.

"Benny," Jessie groaned.

Rob chuckled. "No, Benny, I'm not, but I don't blame you for being suspicious of me." He sighed. "You see," he explained, "I really couldn't tell anyone my identity."

"What made you think the coins would be hidden here in the woods?" Aunt Jane asked.

"Well, it was a hunch, really," Rob answered. "To answer that question, I think I'd better start at the beginning."

Aunt Jane and the Aldens nodded and waited, a bit impatiently, for him to go on. Rob leaned against the big granite boulder and continued his story.

"You see, Mr. Withington is a very wealthy and also a very kind man. I always thought that some of the people who worked for him took advantage of his good nature."

"You think someone who worked for him took the coins?" Henry asked.

"Yes," Rob answered. "Even the police strongly believed it was an inside job, and there were a number of possibilities. Mr.

Withington employed a cook, a maid, a housekeeper, a chauffeur, a personal secretary, several gardeners, and an illustrator."

"An illustrator?" Violet asked.

"Yes, she was doing drawings of the coins to be published in a book. The collection was stolen before she could finish."

"Who did Mr. Withington suspect?" Jessie wondered.

"Well, he didn't really suspect anyone at first. He's very trusting," Rob said. "But the police thought the robbery must have been done by someone who knew Mr. Withington's habits extremely well. Nothing but the coins were taken, and nothing else in the house was disturbed.

"When Mr. Withington hired me," Rob went on, "I checked up on all the people who worked for him. The illustrator, the chauffeur, and two of the gardeners had been with him less than a year. All the others have worked for him for a very long time and are like his family."

"Like Mrs. McGregor is to us," Benny

whispered to Jessie. She nodded at her brother.

Rob cleared his throat. "Right after the robbery, the illustrator left rather suddenly. At first, Mr. Withington thought it was because there was no more work for her."

"Do you know anything about her?" Violet asked.

"Mr. Withington showed me a picture of her, since I couldn't interview her as I had the others. Her name was Eliza Fallon. She looked like Angela, but in her picture, she had shorter hair."

"You think Angela and Eliza Fallon are the same person?" Henry asked.

"Yes," Rob said. "When I met her yesterday, I was pretty sure, but I needed some evidence. I tried to follow her, but it was hard with this ankle." Rob looked down at his leg and winced.

"Where did you see her go?" Benny asked.

"When she left the bunkhouse, she went into the woods," Rob said. "She didn't stay long before she headed quickly to her canoe. When I arrived at the lake, she had already taken off. I followed her a bit along the shore then came back to these woods to see if I could find any clues."

"Did you find anything?" Violet asked softly.

"Well, no. It was dark by then and all I had was my flashlight. You're the ones who found something." Rob looked very proud of the Aldens.

"Did you see her take our equipment?" Henry asked.

"No, I didn't." Rob shook his head. "So you see, I still have no solid proof against her."

"That's too bad." Benny looked disappointed.

"How did you know to look for her here?" Aunt Jane asked.

"Mr. Withington told me Angela loved to go canoeing in this part of the country," Rob explained. "She particularly liked to go by the old abandoned house on Timberwolf Lake."

"That's the house we saw on our first night of the trip," Jessie exclaimed.

"So, did Mr. Withington suspect Angela — or Eliza?" Violet asked.

"Well, of all his employees, he finally admitted she was one of the most suspicious. I decided to take a trip up here on a hunch I might find something. It's been almost a year since the coin collection was stolen," Rob said.

"Do you suspect any of the other new employees?" Jessica wondered.

"Well, the two new gardeners are still working for Mr. Withington and seem very honest. The chauffeur, however, suddenly disappeared a few weeks ago."

"What did this chauffeur look like?" Jessie asked.

"He was a big man with blond hair and a loud voice."

"Hey, wait, that sounds like Matt," Benny shouted.

"That's just what I was thinking." Aunt Jane nodded at Benny.

Jessie, Aunt Jane, and Benny told Rob about meeting Matt and Bill in the storm. They also told him about Lorenzo Espinosa.

Rob listened closely. "We always thought more than one person might be involved in stealing that collection. I wonder. . . " His voice trailed off.

"What do you think we should do now?" Henry asked.

"We should try to get these coins safely to the nearest town — White Pine, I believe," Rob answered.

"That's where we're meeting Grand-father," Benny said.

"Good," Rob nodded. "We shouldn't talk to anyone before we get the coins safely into the hands of the police."

When Aunt Jane and the Aldens arrived at the bunkhouse with the coins, they saw smoke coming from the chimney.

"Look, there are some other campers here." Violet sounded worried.

"Jessie and I will take the coins and hide them," Rob said. "We don't want to take any chances."

Henry slowly opened the door.

"Well, hello again!" a loud voice greeted them. Matt and Bill were seated on the couch in front of the fireplace. Both of them were covered with red blisters.

"I see you found your family." Bill nodded toward Violet and Henry.

"You must have been bitten by lots of mosquitoes," Benny observed.

"We camped in some poison ivy," Matt said ruefully as he scratched his arm.

"Say, you wouldn't happen to have any lotion we could put on it?" Bill asked.

"No." Aunt Jane shook her head. "We didn't bring any."

"Didn't you know to avoid it?" Benny asked.

"Yes, but . . . uh — " Bill started.

"It doesn't matter," Matt said. "We're heading for home this afternoon anyway. We don't want to do any more camping for a while."

"Oh, did you finish mapping the canoe routes already?" Aunt Jane asked.

Matt and Bill looked at one another. Bill even stopped scratching his arm. They seemed to have no idea what she was referring to. "Yes, we did," Matt finally answered.

"We should really be going," Bill said with a pointed look at Matt.

"Yes," Matt agreed, a little too quickly. "It was good to rest here by the fire awhile. So long."

"Good-bye," the Aldens called as Matt and Bill went out the door.

"I wonder what that was all about," Aunt Jane said, puzzled.

"Why did they even come in the bunkhouse and build a fire, if they were planning to leave right away?" Violet asked.

"Maybe they didn't expect us to be here." Henry bent down to tie the shoelaces on his sneakers.

"Didn't you say they were park rangers?" Violet asked.

"That's what they told us," said Aunt Jane.

"I can't believe that two rangers would camp in poison ivy," Violet pointed out.

"Even I know better than that!" added Benny.

At that moment, Rob and Jessie came in.

"Matt and Bill were just here, but they had to go," Benny explained.

"Yes, I know. We saw them leave," Rob answered. "I recognized one of them. He was Mr. Withington's chauffeur."

"Where are the coins?" Henry asked.

"They're right here." Rob pulled the brown leather pouch from the inside pocket of his jacket. "We decided it was safer to keep them with us."

"Do you think they left because we were here?" Benny asked.

"I don't know, Benny. I just hope they don't make any trouble for us before we get to White Pine," Rob said grimly.

CHAPTER 10

The Rapids

"I hope we made the right decision to leave tomorrow instead of right away," Jessie said worriedly.

The Aldens and Rob were seated around the fireplace in the bunkhouse, eating dinner. They planned to leave very early the next morning for White Pine.

"Jessie, look at the weather," Henry said. He scraped the last bit of beef stew off his plate. "We couldn't have gotten very far in all this rain."

"I just hope we won't run into Angela or

Matt." Violet frowned. She put her plate down and curled up on the soft rug in front of the fire.

Aunt Jane yawned. "After we clean up, I think we should stop worrying and go to bed," she said. "Remember, we have to be up very early tomorrow."

The sun was just rising when Aunt Jane and the Aldens pushed their canoes into the lake the next morning. Aunt Jane had assured Henry they would be all right using just one paddle for each canoe.

Henry sat in the back of his canoe. To keep it on course, he paddled first on the left, then on the right, then on the left again. Aunt Jane did the same in her canoe.

Rob carried the coin collection with him. He sat in Henry's canoe behind Violet.

By noon, the two canoes reached the small rapids. "I can't believe this is the last part of the trip already," Benny said. He sounded sad.

"Just be glad we've found the coins and so far no one has bothered us," Jessie said.

"I'm afraid you spoke too soon." Aunt Jane pointed in front of them. Up ahead, they saw a large wooden canoe with red lettering on the sides. It was Angela!

"Oh no," Jessie groaned. "Henry, look up ahead!" she called to the other canoe.

Rob rummaged in his day pack for his binoculars. "She's alone," he said. "We'll be all right."

"She may not even know we have the coins," Violet said.

"Let's stop here for a minute," Aunt Jane called to Henry. She wanted to study the rapids.

"Look, Henry. See how small the waves are? That means the current isn't very strong. We'll be all right, even with just one paddle for each canoe."

"Yes." Rob smiled at Henry. "Just keep the canoe going in the same direction as the current and we'll be fine."

Aunt Jane took the lead. Henry followed.

"Hey, this is fun!" Benny exclaimed. Small waves splashed against the canoe and sprayed his face.

He looked back at Henry's canoe. He could see that Henry, Violet, and Rob were enjoying the rapids, too. Then he looked ahead for Angela's canoe.

Already, they had caught up to her. Her canoe had too much equipment in it and was riding very low in the water. When she went over the rapids, a lot of water went into her canoe. It sank lower and lower.

While Benny watched, Angela's canoe hit a rock under the water and rolled over. She was thrown out into the current.

"Help! Help!" she screamed.

"Aunt Jane, Henry, look!" Benny yelled.

Henry had already seen what had happened. He headed his canoe toward the shore. Aunt Jane followed.

Angela was in the water, struggling against the current.

"Angela!" Henry yelled from the shore. "Try to get to that rock!" He didn't know if she heard him or not. She may have had the same idea because she slowly swam to the big gray boulder and clung to it.

Henry waded into the water and threw her

a long rope. After several tries, Angela finally caught it. She clung to the rope while Henry and Rob pulled her in to the shore.

Angela's knees and elbows were bleeding. Her face was bruised. She shivered from the cold water.

Jessie grabbed a sleeping bag to wrap around her. Aunt Jane and Violet found bandages in the first-aid kit and put them on her worst cuts. Rob gave her hot coffee from his thermos.

"My canoe, can you save my canoe?" Angela asked.

"I'm afraid not," Rob answered. "Your canoe was swept downstream."

"But all my equipment was in it," Angela said in despair. "I've lost everything."

"Well, at least you're alive and not too badly hurt," Rob said gently.

"Yes." Angela nodded. "Thanks to you all. You've been nicer to me than I deserve after the way I've treated you," she said.

"What do you mean?" Rob asked.

"Well, I tried to scare you all away. I didn't want anyone to find. . . ."

"Find what, Angela?" Rob prodded her a little.

"Oh, never mind. I'm not myself right now." Angela became quiet.

Everyone could see Angela was very tired. No one had the heart to ask her any more questions.

Angela changed into some of Aunt Jane's dry clothes. When she was ready, the others bundled her into Henry's canoe and headed quickly for White Pine.

"We should get you to a doctor," Violet told her.

Angela shrugged. "I'm not badly hurt," she said.

When they arrived at the dock in White Pine, they were met by Grandfather, the local sheriff, and Lorenzo Espinosa.

"Grandfather!" Benny ran to him and was swept up in a big bear hug.

"It's good to see you!" Grandfather smiled warmly.

"Your grandfather was worried about you. A motorist just reported a canoeing accident in the rapids," the sheriff explained.

"Yes, I was afraid something had happened to you." Grandfather gave Benny another hug.

"I was worried, too," Lorenzo said. He looked very happy to see the Aldens again. "I was in town filing a report with the sheriff about all the strange happenings in the woods," he explained.

"Oh, Grandfather, we have so much to tell you!" Benny exclaimed.

"So I gather." Grandfather ruffled Benny's hair. "Lorenzo was just telling me about some of your adventures."

"I see something *did* happen to one of your party." The sheriff nodded toward Angela. Rob and Henry were helping her out of the canoe onto the dock. Angela still held Jessie's blue sleeping bag around her shoulders.

"I'll need to ask all of you some questions about the accident," the sheriff said. He gently led Angela to a big wooden picnic table by the dock. The others followed.

Angela told the sheriff her canoe had hit a rock and tipped over. She praised Aunt

Jane, the Aldens, and even Rob for rescuing her. "They saved my life," she said. She looked as if she were near tears.

When the sheriff finished his questioning, Rob turned toward him. "I'm a private detective," Rob explained. He showed the sheriff his detective's license. Angela stared at it with her mouth wide open.

"I would like to turn in a valuable coin collection these children found on their canoe trip." Rob pulled the brown leather pouch from his jacket pocket. "It's Mr. Orville Withington's collection."

The sheriff nodded. "I know about that case."

Angela gasped and turned very pale. "How did you ever find it?" she sputtered.

"What do you know about this?" the sheriff asked sharply.

Angela didn't answer. Instead, she put her hands in front of her face and burst into tears. She cried for a long time. Jessie quietly handed her some tissues. Everyone else looked a little uncomfortable.

When she began to calm down, the sheriff said, "I'm going to have to ask you some more questions." He pulled out his notebook. Angela nodded and gulped.

"I stole Mr. Withington's collection," she began in a low quavery voice. "Matt — Mr. Withington's chauffeur — and I had planned the robbery for a long time." Angela sniffed and blew her nose.

"So you are Eliza Fallon," Rob said.

Angela nodded. "Yes, that's a made-up name. My real name is Angela Tripp."

"How did the coins end up in the woods?" the sheriff asked.

Angela sighed and hugged Jessie's sleeping bag more tightly around her shoulders. "Matt helped me steal the coins," she began. "I hid them in the woods and wrote a riddle on the big boulder as a signal. Matt and his brother Bill were to find the coins and smuggle them out of the country."

"Why did you split up like that?" Jessie couldn't resist asking.

"We didn't want anybody to know we

were in this robbery together," Angela said.

Rob scratched his red beard. "What went wrong?" he asked.

Angela frowned. "Matt and I were supposed to get married. A few months after the burglary, we had a big fight and broke off our engagement." Angela stopped talking and dabbed her eyes with one of Jessie's tissues.

"So you didn't want Matt and Bill to find the coins?" the sheriff asked.

"No." Angela shook her head forcefully. "I did everything I could to scare them away. I made sure Matt and Bill pitched their tent in poison ivy," she said proudly.

"It worked," Henry said. "The last time we saw them, they both had pretty bad cases."

Angela couldn't help smiling a little.

"Did you try to scare us too?" Benny blurted. He'd been waiting for the right moment to ask Angela about the wolf.

"Yes," Angela nodded. She looked very tired. "I made a tape of wolf calls to scare campers away. I also made lots of campfires at odd hours and I even shined a light in your tent one night, Jessie." Angela sighed heavily before continuing. "I even dug a hole near your tent, Rob."

Rob looked down at his ankle. "It seems to be getting better," was all he said. He exchanged glances with the sheriff.

"I'm afraid you'll have to come with me." The sheriff led Angela away.

CHAPTER 11

Mr. Withington

The following day, Grand-father drove the family station wagon up a long, winding gravel driveway. Ahead, the Aldens could see a very large brick house with white shutters.

A maid met them at the door. She led them to a comfortable living room with a large bay window overlooking a rose garden. A kind-looking gentleman greeted them.

"I'm so happy you came." Mr. Withington shook Grandfather's hand warmly. "Rob told me so much about your family."

Mr. Withington turned to Henry, Jessie, Violet, Benny, and Aunt Jane. "I can't thank you enough for finding my coin collection. It really means so much to me." He beamed at all the Aldens.

Benny was busy looking at a large tray with a chocolate layer cake and strawberries on it. Suddenly, the doorbell rang again. A moment later, the maid came in with Rob.

After greeting everyone, Rob helped himself to some tea from the silver tea set on the piano. Mr. Withington sat in a comfortable armchair by the fireplace. The others settled themselves around him.

Rob reached in his jacket and brought out the leather pouch of coins. "Here they are," he said, handing them to Mr. Withington.

Mr. Withington accepted the coins gratefully, but he looked a little sad just the same. "I still can't really believe Eliza and Matt were responsible for all of this."

"Yes, unfortunately they were." Rob looked sad, too. "They planned this robbery long before they started working here.

They're both wanted for burglary in other states."

"I wonder why they left the coins in the woods in the first place," Jessie said as she helped herself to some lemonade the maid brought.

"They wanted to hide them until all the publicity had died down a bit," Rob explained.

"If Angela knew where the coins were, why didn't she just take them out of their hiding place in the woods after Matt and she broke up?" Henry asked.

"It's almost impossible to travel to Timberwolf Lake in the winter," Rob explained. Mr. Withington nodded. "They had to wait until the spring before they could go and get the coins.

"Besides, Angela is the type of person who likes to play games. She liked the idea of scaring Matt almost as much as she wanted the coins," Rob said.

"She sure did a good job scaring us, too," Benny mentioned. He took the big glass of milk the maid handed him. His glass had little red canoes all over it.

Mr. Withington opened the pouch of coins and spread them out on the coffee table in front of him. Violet picked up a pretty silver coin with a willow tree on it and held it up to the light.

"That was one of the first coins to be minted in the colonies," Mr. Withington explained to her.

Violet smiled at him. "You know," she said, turning to Rob, "I still don't understand how Angela had time to steal all our canoe equipment at the bunkhouse."

"She moved very quickly. She saw you arrive in the canoe and stole everything before she even went to the bunkhouse to meet you." Rob had picked up a large gold doubloon and was examining it.

"She must have thought her job was over with Matt and Bill off the trail," Mr. Withington remarked.

"Yes, she never dreamed she'd have so many people to scare off, this early in the

canoeing season. That was the trouble. She had no time to take the coins out of their hiding place. She never thought some children would be able to find them." Rob smiled at the Aldens.

"What about the attempted robbery in the local museum?" Grandfather wondered. He poured more milk into his tea.

"Oh, Angela did that, too," Rob said. "She thought they might have some rare colonial coins that would add to the value of Mr. Withington's collection."

"Goodness, she thought of almost everything," Mr. Withington said.

"Yes, she even knew where Matt and Bill were. We picked them up this morning. They're still itching from their poison ivy," Rob chuckled.

"Will we ever get our camping equipment back?" Benny asked.

"I'm afraid it sank with Angela's canoe," Rob said.

Mr. Withington cleared his throat. "I'm planning to replace the equipment you lost," he said. "It's the least I could do."

"Thank you, Mr. Withington." Violet beamed.

"Ernie will thank you, too," Henry said, smiling.

"Now, why don't you all have something to eat, if you're hungry," Mr. Withington said.

"Oh, I'm always hungry," Benny said. He helped himself to some chocolate cake and took a big bite. "You know, the hot dogs on the trail were good," he said. "But this is much better!"

Everyone laughed.

GERTRUDE CHANDLER WARNER discovered when she was teaching that many readers who like an exciting story could find no books that were both easy and fun to read. She decided to try to meet this need, and her first book, *The Boxcar Children*, quickly proved she had succeeded.

Miss Warner drew on her own experiences to write the mystery. As a child she spent hours watching trains go by on the tracks opposite her family home. She often dreamed about what it would be like to set up housekeeping in a caboose or freight car — the situation the Alden children find themselves in.

When Miss Warner received requests for more adventures involving Henry, Jessie, Violet, and Benny Alden, she began additional stories. In each, she chose a special setting and introduced unusual or eccentric characters who liked the unpredictable.

While the mystery element is central to each of Miss Warner's books, she never thought of them as strictly juvenile mysteries. She liked to stress the Aldens' independence and resourcefulness and their solid New England devotion to using up and making do. The Aldens go about most of their adventures with as little adult supervision as possible — something else that delights young readers.

Miss Warner lived in Putnam, Connecticut, until her death in 1979. During her lifetime, she received hundreds of letters from girls and boys telling her how much they liked her books.